In Rare Case
Unfortunate Circumstances

Coleman Bigelow

abuddhapress@yahoo.com

ISBN: 9798393106218

Coleman Bigelow 2023

®™©

Alien Buddha Press 2023

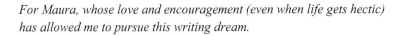

For Maura, whose love and encouragement (even when life gets hectic) has allowed me to pursue this writing dream.

For Molly, Ian & Maeve, who remind me every day of life's potential.

And for my parents who instilled in me the love of a story well told.

SIBLINGS

Xan & Grit

Long before the children would shed their gender conforming names and escape their provincial village, the two siblings endured a tortuous childhood of stifling convention. The children's mother called her son Hansel, a 'healthy eater' and her daughter, Gretel, a 'little piggy.' Their father clapped Hansel on his meaty back and offered him a stein of the family pilsner, while their mother showed Gretel how to polish the silver and iron the wrinkles out of lederhosen.

One day when the children's father was at the pretzel factory and their mother was busy churning butter, Gretel went to Hansel's room to borrow a hammer and steal some of his chocolate. Hansel always seemed to have chocolate stashed around his room. When Gretel pushed open the door, she found her brother dressed in an elaborate dirndl. He was radiant, and at that moment, Gretel knew they were destined for better lives.

As their authentic identities emerged from saccharine chrysalides, it was "Auf wiedersehen!" to Hansel & Gretel and "Willkommen!" to Xan & Grit. The children immediately began

9

scanning *Rolf's List* for a place where they could no longer pretend.

After several weeks of searching, Grit spotted an intriguing ad:

"Do you want to get away from it all?

Do you like unlimited candy?

Are you open to creative architecture?

If you're willing to put in a little sweat equity for free room and board,

then please call 1-800-EAT-SWEET.

This is a stigma-free cottage."

As soon as she finished reading, Grit circled the ad and thrust it in front of her brother's Black Cherry mascara painted eyes.

"Vut do you tink?" she asked, unable to hide her excitement.

"Vut's not to like?" Xan replied, spinning so his skirt fluttered upward in the cool Bavarian breeze.

VOTE HERE

The fine red hairs on my brother's pale forearm shimmer in the sharp November light. The muscles underneath his skin ripple and flex as he grips and guides the steering wheel. Aaron is our proud driver. He comes home from college often now that he has his own car.

My stomach churns as the old Taurus rocks over a speed bump and we arrive at our destination. 'Our destiny' mother calls it. Aaron parks in the shade of a brilliant maple whose leaves are coloring over but have yet to drop. I can already hear the shouting outside. They're lined up on either side of the entrance. Everywhere I look is an assault of wombs and fetuses.

"Now don't you pay any attention to those murderers, Miriam. This is your moment, and it's a blessing. Your first vote and you're able to do God's work." I smile and wipe my cheek. Papa opens the door and takes mother's hand. Aaron comes to my door and waits expectantly.

I hold my breath as we walk, but soon the screams and flapping posters are behind us. We're in the cool of the school cafeteria. I smell bleach and Tater Tots and my eyes search for the

11

nearest garbage can. As we wait, I think of all the dances held here and what it must be like to be embraced by some handsome classmate.

When my time comes, my black flats slip on the scuffed white linoleum. It's warm inside the booth and I can feel the weighty thumping of my heart. I stare at the ballot. A version of the same ballot my mother carefully pinned on my bulletin board, positioned just below the cross Papa carved. And I want so desperately to save lives. To vote yes.

It's a sin to murder, I know. But then I think of Leviticus and what Aaron and I have done. I think of the sin that lives inside me.

Estranged

Would you rather die by burning or drowning? I think those are our basic choices these days. Personally, I can't understand why my sister, Marnie, would choose burning, but she says the West Coast's lack of humidity is better for her hair.

I don't want to burn. I'd rather be swept away in the torrential rains of the East Coast. Drowning seems more peaceful. I can picture my pale body bobbing up and down in a gully wash of river brown. I might struggle to breathe, but once I resign myself and accept my watery fate, at least I won't be in pain. Much better than slowly cooking to death.

Why Marnie would abandon the East Coast, I'll never understand. The floods and the bugs are getting worse, but tell me a place that isn't struggling. Besides, our family goes back generations in Ulster County. And we've been growing our own food long before it was fashionable. There was a time when Marnie took pride in that. When she seemed to cherish milking the cows and gathering the eggs. But as she grew older and prettier, she had no patience for a small-town farm. She wanted less work and more money. Lobbied for shortcuts and outsourcing: insecticides and milking machines.

Looking back, I wonder if she was always secretly embarrassed by us. By me. She lives to stand out. Even had the nerve to be born with blonde hair, while I got stuck with mousy brown. I thought we'd remain close, no matter where she went, but that was before she published her novel. It was bad enough on the page but, once book became film, my 'fictional' life was easy access for anyone to consume. I suppose I should give Marnie credit for recycling, but some things are better left to compost.

Now she's living the West Coast cliché: lighting grip husband, who's really an aging surfer, and three tan beach babies who've never met their aunt. Marnie barely even stayed after Mom's funeral. Preferred to breeze in and out like the shifting Santa Anas. And after my divorce, all she did was send flowers. Seriously, what am I supposed to do with flowers in an empty house? Not to mention the life cycle impact of growing, cutting and shipping all that organic waste. Flowers I could step outside and pick myself.

Some might say we should meet in the middle - both move near our brother Luke's house in Minnesota. I've heard the lake country may fare best with climate change. But why prolong the inevitable? Plus, Luke is a hunter now. Sans husband and offspring (you're welcome, Mother Earth), I imagine I'd be conscripted into being a gatherer out there. Because isn't that what we're reverting back to? The world coming to an end and we're all just Neanderthals once more. Struggling to survive before the harsh environment snuffs out our flame.

Yeah, it's the Ophelia route for me. No sense waiting to be burned again.

LOVERS

Summer Catch

The curtains floated inward like ghosts as I walked the wide oak planks to the foot of the bed. The wrought iron bed somehow incomplete without Deirdre's boots beside it. Those boots, so incongruous to this part of the Cape, they caught my attention. One heel resting provocatively on a stool's middle rung. Glimpses of freckled legs between boots and skirt and red hair spilling over bare shoulders. I sat mesmerized as she tipped a Bud Light to her lips, then laughed at something Jimmy, the bartender, said. One of those opportunistic Emerald Islers drawn by the cash-crop of summer folk.

I'd come with someone else. My usual catch. A tourist from my charter boat. A preppy college girl who wanted a chance with the sunburned local and was willing to overlook the lingering smell of fish. I didn't mind being a fling, someone she could tell her fancy friends about. I didn't even mind that my date kept glancing at another guy on the dance floor with a braided belt and loafers. Until I saw Deirdre.

Blaming my departure on an early morning start, I followed Deirdre outside. I found her blowing smoke into the fog and reached for her cigarette.

17

"Aren't you forward," she teased, in that erotic Irish lilt. She watched with amusement as I took a long draw. "Your date doesn't smoke?"

I passed her cigarette back. "She's just a friend."

"So, what will you tell her when you leave with me?"

At my grandparent's house, I gave Deirdre a beer and a tour of the cottage. "Oh, I love this bed," she said ducking under the eaves to caress the black iron twists on the frame.

"I'm glad you like it," I said moving closer. "I like your boots."

"Ta," she said sitting on the bed and raising a leg. "Aren't they exquisite? I got them in Kentucky."

For the rest of the season, we were inseparable. Deirdre nannying city brats, and me leading charters for the best fishing money could buy. We shared a disdain for the summer people, regaled each other with stories of their daily embarrassments. And when they were gone, we swam naked, the sunsets ours alone.

I started to believe I might marry this girl – that our shared work ethic would propel us to new heights. My Aunt, a realtor who grew more like the summer people with each house she sold, chided "She's too good for you" but I knew she was also charmed.

As the days grew shorter, Deirdre persuaded me to come home with her to Ireland for Christmas. It was only when we turned down the driveway to her family's estate that I realized she wasn't like me at all.

"I hadn't intended to stay so long...until I met you," she whispered while her parents sidestepped me as if I was something rotten just washed ashore. "The money was good," she said flipping her hair, "but that's not what's most important." Easy for you to say I thought.

How did I miss the signs of polish? The thick paperbacks she toted to the beach, the expensive toiletries filling my bathroom shelves. I'd been her own summer catch. Certainly no match for a girl who rode horses and attended Trinity. And there was no school waiting for me, only the endless expanse of blue.

Returning home in bleak January, I discovered my aunt had convinced my parents to sell. They were headed to Florida and the lure of Marlins. I would have fought to hold onto the house for Deirdre but, now, it was just a tear-me-down for some rich schmuck. I wondered if

they'd keep the bed. It wouldn't be easy to move.

Mistress #19

You aren't positive you're a couple until you find it hard to breathe. She sweeps in, magnificent in her mutability. You might have met her on the plane, attending that long-delayed concert or during your first trip back to the movies. You weren't looking, but it's hard to deny you were open to the possibilities. For months you wore protection, but then you wondered what was the point. You slipped up, and she was there to catch you.

Now, you cannot shake her. A few of your friends claim she's nothing more than a silent hitchhiker. Some don't even notice her until they hear the car door slam at a stoplight downtown. Until they spot a sultry specter in the rearview mirror, a shadow streaking by under the overpass.

But you, you always knew she was there. Your punctured oil pan evidence enough—mysterious black pools collecting nightly beneath your overheated engine. At first you struggle, but her fiery hands burn your leather stitching and your tires shudder in the rumble strip. Once in control, she tightens her grip until your mind grows muddy.

21

You flutter in and out of consciousness and find yourself parked somewhere in purgatory–Netflix, the only thing you recognize. Your willpower overwhelmed; she infects you with her Real Housewives. You slumber and sweat and beg for her departure, but still she lingers.

A concerned friend suggests therapy, but you doubt your relationship even qualifies. So, you lay with her until, at last, she grows bored of your coughing. You hear her slip from the sheets, and you silently rejoice. Whisper hallelujahs at her naked back. Your celebrations are muted, however, for even as slivers of your former self reappear, you fret about her return. She's changed her look before, and she's already proven impossible to resist.

Do Not Associate

The tests, which seemed an exciting next step in their relationship, now appeared to mark their final chapter as a couple. The likelihood of their children being born with a terminal disease tripled by a shared mutation in their DNA.

Evangeline wished she'd never suggested the test for genetic compatibility. Abel had resisted, but she'd explained her friend could get them access to diagnostics which would have been otherwise cost prohibitive. It was too good an offer to refuse, except now it devastated her to have been the one who pushed. He was kind; he tried to make light of it. If they'd wanted to see the future, he said, "they should have just gone to Madame Portia down the street."

For all he joked, she could tell he was upset. If they stayed together, there should be children—just like they'd said they wanted in their online profiles. Abel maintained, with brow furrowed, they "could overcome almost any medical challenge", and Evangeline had concurred "because babies defy the odds all the time." Neither of them sounded convinced or convincing.

Still, it was hard to deny the fit of their bodies. His chin resting on her head as her knee tucked between his thighs. The feeling in her fingers as she traced the ripple of his spine. The undeniable current that cycled between them. Even the discovery of their complementary strengths in trivia had been a thrill. She'd delighted in their domination at Putnam's Pub—Evangeline handling History and Entertainment, while Abel shouldered Arts & Leisure and Geography. They had almost all wedges covered. And yet they weren't a full pie, especially not when their ingredients shared a hidden rot.

Evangeline didn't want to stop seeing Abel, but he was already forty-three. She'd read somewhere that older fathers had higher rates of autistic children. Then, at thirty-eight, there was her own advanced maternal age to consider and the notion of the dreaded geriatric pregnancy. Complications loomed: preeclampsia, or other equally frightening sounding conditions. But Abel was worth the risk... wasn't he?

As they lounged in bed on a Sunday morning, she thought of how complicated life would be with a child and then she thought of how much more complicated it would be with a sick child. She rolled onto her side and propped her head on her fist. He lay on his back, his chest hair peeking out from the top of a white sheet. His eyes, normally inviting, now less so.

"Well, what do you think?" she asked, trying to draw his attention. "We could always adopt," she said, forcing a smile. "Isn't that less selfish, anyway?"

"It's a possibility," he said before placing his thick forearm over his eyes. The skin on the underside of his arm was pale and hairless. Beneath the surface, blue veins raced like icy rivers down to his curled palm. And there, lurking in the shadows of his hand, was a hidden fortune waiting to be read.

PARENTS

Dancers

Dan and Susan sat in silence at their corner table by the window. The food had been good but the place too formal, and Dan regretted this choice for their last vacation meal. He half-heartedly contemplated a dessert menu before looking up to see Susan's profile backlit by the setting sun. She smiled open mouthed—animated in a way he hadn't seen for months—and he turned to find what had captured her attention.

Just outside, on the lawn leading down to the harbor, two children, a tall thin girl who looked about ten and a husky red-cheeked boy, maybe two years her junior, were in the middle of a spontaneous dance-off. Both children danced to imagined beats, but it was clear they grooved to different tunes. One bopped, and the other bounced, one spun, and the other jumped and gyrated. The girl more studied, while the boy shifted from wild hip thrusting to rowdy butt shaking, his arms flying up and down to accentuate each move. The boy reminded Dan of one of his students from the previous year. A boy he was constantly disciplining but secretly found amusing. A boy whose exploits he had enjoyed sharing with Susan, when she was still excited to hear such stories.

Inside the restaurant, the dancers attracted a growing audience. A man two tables away slapped his leg with laughter as he watched the boy execute a dance move that involved riding an imaginary pony. Susan giggled and, listening to her, Dan thought of how the shock of her convulsive laughter had first attracted him. He loved the progression of her laugh from quiet snicker to full throated guffaw. The magical surprise of this otherwise-graceful person letting go. A laugh that had faded from Dan's world like a close school friend you don't realize you miss until you run into them again on the street years later. A friend with whom you are instantly able to reconnect. A friend to whom you would confide about the baby.

It was growing dark, but the children gravitated to a pool of fading sunlight. The girl appeared to explain some rules to the boy and then, after a dramatic pause, began her own elaborate routine. She clapped her hands and did a kind of grapevine back and forth. Then she stopped, put her hands to her sides and jumped to cross one leg in front of the other. Once in position, she spun herself around while pivoting on crossed feet in a perfect Michael Jackson imitation. She finished by dropping into a split.

With a satisfied smile, she motioned to the boy to take his turn. The boy appeared stumped, but then clapped his hands over his head and rotated his hips. He did a running in place routine that made his stomach jiggle inside his t-shirt. Dan noticed the girl purse her lips as the boy shot fake guns from his fingertips. The boy laughed and spun around the girl, eluding her grasp. Mid-rotation, he froze and pointed at the restaurant.

The children, eyes widening, registered all the faces looking down. The girl gasped. She pulled the boy in the direction of the guest cabins. Halfway up the hill, the boy broke free to sneak one more peek at the diners. He took an impromptu bow and grinned, his broad smile stretching his chubby cheeks. Dan put one hand on the glass and watched as the boy caught up with the girl and disappeared into the shadows.

After the children's departure, chairs were rotated back into tables and the steady buzz of conversation resumed. Dan missed the distraction of the children—the escape from the unspoken. He was tired. Tired of waiting for her. He'd begun to wonder if she'd ever be ready again. Susan continued to stare into the fading light. She sipped her tea. The same tea she had nursed throughout dinner, frequently lifting the little white pot to refill her cup even as the water grew cold. Susan had taken to drinking tea after their baby died.

"Good dinner?" Dan asked, reaching for her hand.

"Those kids were the highlight," she replied, and moved her hands to her lap.

A final splash of pink retreated across the harbor lawn.

"Free entertainment," Dan said, finishing his last drop of bourbon.

Susan twisted the napkin in her lap. "You forget how uninhibited kids are at that age."

"Or how much joy they can bring." Dan said. Her eyes locked onto his. The blacks of her pupils first expanding and then shrinking as if absorbing the subtext. Dan smoothed the tablecloth in front of him. "Isn't it time?"

Susan's full lips squeezed tighter. She nodded. "I didn't think I'd ever be ready, but…" She paused and pushed herself up. "Can you pay the check while I run to the ladies?" Midway across the floor, she glanced over her shoulder, and Dan wondered if she was happy he was still watching her or wishing he would look away.

You Drunk

You'll be speeding, oblivious to anything other than your push-in lighter and your pint of SoCo. You won't spot me stepping out. You'll be too busy belching out some song and breezing past those spindly trees, oblivious to the specter of your crouching broken boy. You'll blame the dark. You'll tell the trooper there was no way you could have detected some kid hiding in black jeans and a hoodie. But the hoodie you've just left tire tracks on is the same one you gave me last Christmas. A Goodwill hoodie that cost you less than a bucket of beer.

Gator Baby

Doreen had always wanted to be a mother until she became one. It didn't help that she'd failed to have the natural birth she planned or that she'd been allergic to her epidural. Her hallucinations had magnified with each contraction, and the hospital room pulsed with a series of deafening screams. In time, Doreen discerned that the wailing was issuing from her own mottled neck as she heaved and moaned and watched her drenched body from somewhere above.

As awful as the baby's birthing had been, the passing pain had, in no way, compared to the convulsive shock that came with the baby's arrival. Doreen remembered the nurse telling her the baby was breech, but not to worry, because "it will be easier to pull the tail this way." Soon a baby alligator emerged, its little snout snapping, its spiky torso flipping and wriggling. And Doreen heard the nurse's clucking, "It's a girl... and a feisty one at that!"

Doreen couldn't understand why her husband, Leo, wasn't equally disgusted by their grotesque offspring. But Leo was smitten, and he promised Doreen that once they got the baby home, things would improve. Only being home made no difference, and Doreen felt herself slipping - sliding down the sewer drain. Her residence post-baby was a murky cave from which she could find no exit. She knew there was light somewhere above, but the manhole was too heavy to lift. She huddled in the dank, dark depths of motherhood, sleepwalking through much of her day, until the bellowing alligator came to feed. Doreen tried to escape by wading through the knee-deep muck, but every few hours, her persistent predator wrestled her under the surface. It was futile to resist the sharp teeth tearing at her tender nipples. The alligator would have its fill.

At night, the hissing of the rats and roaches reverberated throughout her subterranean prison. "You're *not the one* who belongs here," they cried. Doreen had a foggy desire that Leo would come to pull her back into the light, just as Orpheus had come for Eurydice. Except when Leo did appear, he came seeking only the alligator. Leo was content to leave Doreen wallowing while he cradled the gator and tipped formula into its pointy snout. Separated by a growing chasm, Doreen listened as Leo cooed over that intrusive reptile.

Eventually, she grew tired of the stink. She shed her partum covers and stepped into a scalding shower. Emerging grime-free for the first time in weeks, Doreen resolved to reclaim her role as matriarch and reestablish the order of her above-ground lair.

And she did fine… for a while.

She played peek-a-boo with the baby the way she knew other mothers did. She took the baby for long walks along the muddy banks of the river. She pureed peas and carrots and watched the growing gator snap them down like flushed goldfish. She even read aloud *The Hungry Caterpillar* until all the book's thick pages had been chewed through. For a few hopeful weeks, Doreen dreamed her baby would transform like the caterpillar in the story. Still, the more time she spent with the gator, the more she was repulsed. The creature's scales were hardening alongside her heart.

While she could find no love for the baby, Doreen still harbored a strong yearning for her husband. She was desperate to recapture Leo's attention—to remind him of the woman he'd once loved more than any crawling interloper. She dieted and did sit-ups. She flat-ironed her hair and put on makeup. But Leo's eye had wandered… it was now fixed permanently on their ravenous daughter.

When he did glance Doreen's way, all Leo could say was, "You look tired. Why don't you try sleeping in the guest room?"

Doreen knew she would never again feel like herself. Not with that cold-blooded creature moving in their midst. So, one afternoon at bath-time, she took charge. As her tormentor squirmed and flailed in the frothy suds, Doreen held the reptile down and waited until its tail stopped thrashing. The sudden quiet in the bath seemed to echo off the tile. Doreen had never known silence as a sound, but she welcomed the reprieve.

MOURNERS

Shots

"What are you worried about? That kid Messi took the stuff," Meg's dad said, thwacking the pamphlet with the back of his thick fingers. "And now he's the star of Barcelona."

"But she's only eight," her mother replied, glancing nervously at Meg.

"And she's already fallen off the growth curve, Ruth. She needs this."

Meg was used to being at the center of their arguments, even when she knew they weren't really fighting about her.

"What if she gets hurt?"

"She'll take the shots after practice," her father said, rubbing Meg's arm. "That way, she won't be sore."

Meg didn't think of herself as small and she hated needles, but she loved her dad.

***

37

Meg was listening to her Walkman so didn't hear him enter. She turned to discover her father, standing behind her, his brow furrowed.

"Get out!" she shrieked throwing down the Victoria's Secret catalogue and yanking off her pink headphones. Her father stepped back slowly. He'd seen her studying Heidi Klum in the floral lace teddy; she was sure of it by the look on his face.

"What!?," she asked indignant, as her father's gaze bore into her. "You can't just sneak up on me like that."

Her father hovered in the doorway, backlit by the hallway light, a slender shadow of a man in his uniform of khakis and a button down.

"You should be studying, Meg. If you don't get your scores up, you won't have any chance at Stanford… or even UNC. The recruiters can't do everything."

Meg couldn't face him. Stared instead at the Team USA poster of Mia Hamm, with her perfect smile. She'd wanted Brandi Chastain ripping off her jersey, but her mother said that was unladylike.

"I know you think I push you too hard, but this is your shot, honey. This is your shot at something better."

Something better than what, Meg wanted to ask, but her father had already stepped out of the room. Her dad hadn't been particularly athletic yet somehow, he expected more from her.

***

Tiny flecks of gold swam inside twenty-one celebratory shot glasses and she drank them down one by one. A country song came on and everyone in the bar started to sing along. Cinnamon tingled and burned inside Meg's mouth. "Only fourteen more to go," her teammate, Jane, whispered in Meg's ear. Jane's hot breath was a mix of menthol and beer. As Meg swallowed another tiny glass of trouble, something lurched inside her. She dropped off the barstool and winced as her full weight came down on her left knee. It was too soon after the ACL surgery to be out. But how often did you turn twenty-one? She steadied herself against the bar.

"You alright there, sweetie?" the bartender asked. She nodded and waited for him to leave. His condescending care reminded Meg of her father. *"You could lose your scholarship, if you're not careful. Then you'll never go pro."*

39

"I don't give a fuck," Meg said, wiping a bit of drool from her mouth and smudging ruby-red lipstick across the back of her hand. Jane hugged her from behind. "Cheers to that."

***

Her father's heart attack was both crushing and liberating at the same time and it made Meg dizzy to think she now only had one parent left to disappoint. Locked inside her parents' bathroom, Meg dabbed at a stain on her black dress. She looked as if she'd been shot. She felt as if she'd been shot. In search of some aspirin, Meg discovered, instead, a bottle of Prozac with her mother's name: *Ruth Ruffino.*

With the house finally empty of mourners, Meg found her mother rearranging something in the refrigerator. Her mother jumped when Meg touched her shoulder. "How are you holding up?"

"I'm happy they're all gone."

Meg wondered what else she didn't know about her mother.

"Your father would have been pleased. It was a good turnout."

"Mom. I'm asking about you."

Ruth stared at Meg, her eyes vacant and endless, like two dying stars. "It was nice to meet your friend Emma." She continued to transfer lasagna into Tupperware. "Can she introduce you to anyone?"

Meg wanted to hug her mother, and to slap her, but instead she took out the garbage.

***

Ruth sat, shoulders stooped, at the kitchen table of Meg's rented Baltimore row house.

"I thought I heard gunfire last night."

"You probably did," Meg said pouring herself more coffee.

"Oh, Meg," Ruth smoothed her skirt and took a sip of the wheatgrass juice she always brought. "It's not safe."

"It's close to Hopkins."

"Your father wouldn't have liked to see you living like this."

"I think Dad would have been proud." The longer he'd been gone, the more Meg believed it. It wasn't just about being better, it had always been about being her best.

Ruth's eyes widened, but then she nodded. "When you get engaged, you'll get some money…"

41

"Who says I want to get engaged?"

Ruth wiped crumbs from the table into her cupped hand and moved to drop them in the sink. "I didn't say 'engaged to a man'."

Meg's legs buckled. She braced herself against her mother's vacated chair, then sat. She stared at the back of her mother's tidy gray bob. Watched as Ruth washed the crumbs down the drain.

"What do you mean, Mom?"

Ruth turned, her wrinkled mouth opening into a warm smile. "I mean, I want you to be happy."

After an extended farewell, Meg watched her as mother's rusting Volvo pulled away. A newfound fondness swept over her. She cleared her mother's glass and the smell of mown grass wafted up. It was a smell that made Meg want to pull on her cleats and go practice her shot. Not for her father, or for anyone else, but only to discover what she had left for herself.

Clearing House

Gram's house is rotting. The front porch sags to the ground like it's taking some woeful last curtain call. I've never considered this place my father's, and I don't now consider it my own. All that's left is an unpaid mortgage and a happy scattering of childhood memories when the place was still filled with possibility.

***

"Did you get yours?" my grandmother's voice croaked from the receiver.

"This is our year." Mom would promise her mother-in-law while twisting the long green phone cord around her finger and surveying the contents of a fat orange Publishers Clearing House envelope. "One of us is finally going to hit," she'd say, taking a drag on her Virginia Slim and blowing the smoke out the screen door.

When Mom first got hooked on the notion of winning, Dad threatened to throw her out if he ever caught her ordering anything. Still, I was certain our life would be better with sharper knives, brighter flashlights, and collector's sets of vintage money, and I figured Dad would come around when Ed McMahon knocked on the door. It was hard not to believe in the coming of McMahon, the way my Gram carried on. She bought almost every magazine and talked about winning non-stop.

"You don't have to subscribe to win!" my father often scolded his mother, to no avail. Dad hadn't had a steady job since he got laid off by the pulp mill, and he must have resented Gram spending what he saw as his rightful inheritance. He was constantly rolling his eyes at the piles of magazines, from *National Geographic* to *The National Enquirer,* that covered every surface of her house. My Grandmother hadn't traveled much, but those magazines were her ticket to explore.

The day after I turned thirteen, Mom and I were over at Gram's house. It was a warm spring night, and you could smell the lilacs blooming. We were all kind of edgy because we knew it was right around the time when they'd be walking around with those oversized checks. Then, all of a sudden, Dad came racing through the backyard yelling like there was some kind of fire. Our house was two blocks behind Gram's, and we heard his shouts before we saw him. "Y'all come quick! You need to get back to the house this minute, Pauline." He was panting hard. "There's a camera truck that just pulled up."

Gram and Mom froze. Their rockers stopped mid-rock. Then they both jumped up like they'd been stung and practically threw themselves down that porch's four little stairs. Normally, someone would have held Gram's hand. She was nearing seventy-six with a bad hip, but you wouldn't have known it right then. To watch her flying across those backyards and down those red clay trails that cut between the little row houses of our neighborhood, anyone might have thought she was an Olympic athlete.

As we neared our house, I could see Mom looking up and down the road, her head swiveling like a weather vane in a storm. By that point, Gram had faltered, and I was doing my best to hold her steady. A whistle came from her lungs and the spidery veins in her cheeks pulsed under pale, wrinkled skin.

"Pauline, where they at?" she yelled, still trying to catch her breath.

Mom checked our porch before tearing off again up the street and out of sight. We heard her screaming somewhere down the block, "We're here! The Jenkins family is here!" and Gram and I joined in, adding our voices as I half carried my grandmother toward the front.

"We're here!" Gram was sweating. Rivulets plastered her white hair to her forehead and a wet V had formed at the top of her peach blouse.

"Shit, I hope we didn't miss them," Mom said as she walked back toward us, hands on hips.

"They won't leave if we're the winners." Gram tried to sound optimistic, but she looked wrung out. She flopped down on the front steps of our porch. And, just then, my dad came round the corner, laughing and pointing at Mom and Grandmother.

"You should have seen your faces! Y'all actually believed you won something. How gullible can you get?" He was bent over laughing. It was the first time I noticed the beginnings of a bald spot on his head and I remember thinking: *Good. I hope that asshole loses every last strand of hair.* That was my final thought before Gram collapsed.

They weren't sure if she had the stroke then or later that night, but Gram was never the same after. Mom wanted to get her a full-time nurse, but Dad was too cheap for that. He said we could handle Gram, even though the only time he visited was to clear her place out—throwing away pile after pile of her prized magazines.

***

The front room is bare, Dad's Lazy-Boy the last lone occupant. Staring at the empty chair, I wonder what would have happened if we'd actually won the sweepstakes. Would Mom have left Dad sooner? He'd never been part of our dream, but his reluctance might have been his greatest cruelty. As Gram always said: "You can't win if you don't believe."

In Rare Cases...

You're joking, I say, interrupting the steady bumping of the doctor's bushy white mustache. A mustache that matches his lab coat. And you, my invincible wife, you put your hand to your chest. To the place he's showing us on the X-ray. You're joking, you whisper when the doctor's finished. You're joking, your parents cry, as they arrive and fold you in between them.

Later that night, I curse when I burn my hand on the Pyrex while serving the lasagna. The stiff-noodled lasagna I make which no one eats. What's the matter, Daddy, our little girls ask as we lay on their floor. And we tell them. Our girls. Our family. Our friends. We thought we were done. Except now there's no way to begin. No words to describe. The cure worse than the disease and all that.

The calls flood in, even on our landline. The long-neglected kitchen cordless suddenly ringing back to life. The shrill chiming of a cruel joke. Because in this case, it is. It really is. Because in this case, you're better and then you're not.

Because we didn't hear when Dr. Mustache discussed the treatment the first time around. When he relayed the probabilities and

48

unlikely scenarios. When he kept talking, and we stopped listening. That's when we miss the muttered warnings. His admonitions drifting off like a helium balloon escaping a patient's room only to sit shriveling in an unreachable corner. That was when we missed the risks.

And we celebrated your last successful treatment. We sped away. We lived. And you live. And live and live some more. And at first, it's all more. More kissing. More hugs. More hand holding. More more.

And nothing taken for granted... until. Until it all comes down to the margins.

And you, you're so strong. So brave. So determined.

And you, you're so weak. So scared. So hopeless.

And you, you're so pale. So thin. So sick.

And you. You are. You were.

You're gone.

You're so. So. Gone.

Your sister cleans out your closet and we laugh at your oversized white bunny slippers. White like the doctor's mustache. We laugh. Well, she laughs. And the girls go back to sleeping in their own beds. And I go back to work. And I drive your powder blue CRV because someone tells me it's not good to let it sit.

And I drive that car. I drive the hell out of it. And before I know it, there are flashing lights in the rearview mirror. The officer asks for license and registration. And when I open the glove compartment, all your beautiful mess spills out: coupons and receipts, and a whole bunch of cherry lollipops for your mouth sores. I find the registration and hand it over and, when the officer gives it back, he tells me it's expired. And then he just stands there, looking at me funny, until he finally says, "You're crying."

About the Author:

Coleman Bigelow's flash fiction and short stories have appeared in a wide range of journals. He studied fiction writing and playwriting at The University of Virginia and continues to find inspiration in workshops and seminars across the country. Coleman lives in New Jersey with his wife, three children and two dogs. He's grateful to them all for their support (but especially to the dogs, as they're incredibly insightful readers).

Find more of his recent publications at www.colemanbigelow.com

Made in the USA
Middletown, DE
25 May 2023

31480624R00029